This book belongs to...

_____

© Illus. Dr. Seuss 1957

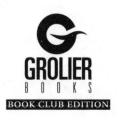

GROLIER
B O O K S
BOOK CLUB EDITION

How the Grinch Got So Grinchy

Published by Grolier Incorporated, 90 Old Sherman Turnpike, Danbury, Connecticut
06816, a subsidiary of Scholastic Inc., by arrangement with Random House, Inc.

GROLIER and associated design is a trademark of Grolier, Inc.

Printed in the United States of America   September 2001   10 9 8 7 6 5 4 3 2 1

RANDOM HOUSE, the Random House colophon, STEP INTO READING, and BEGINNER BOOKS are
registered trademarks and the Step into Reading and Beginner Books colophon are
trademarks of Random House, Inc.

ISBN 0-7172-6554-4

Dr. Seuss'
HOW THE
GRINCH
STOLE
CHRISTMAS!

How the Grinch Got So Grinchy

By Bonnie Worth
Illustrated by Ray Goudey

Based on the motion picture screenplay by
Jeffrey Price & Peter S. Seaman

Based on the book by Dr. Seuss

BEGINNER BOOKS
A Division of Random House, Inc.

Random House 🏠 New York

Unlike the Whos,
who liked Christmas a lot,
the Grinch in his cave
on Mt. Crumpit DID NOT!
"He was born to hate Christmas,"
most people will say.
But maybe his life was
what made him that way.

'Twas the night before Christmas,
quite some time ago.
The night new Who babies
fell down with the snow.
They fell down to earth
on their soft pumbrasellas,
these little Who gals
and these little Who fellas.

The Who parents greeted
each bundle of joy,
except for this one
somewhat sad little boy.

No Who seemed to hear him,
or want him, or need him.
No Who came to hug him,
or clean him, or feed him.

At long last, two Who gals
came out and they found
the source of a most
un-adorable sound.
They got down the baby,
who hung in a tree.
They pulled back the blanket...
and what did they see?

A fuzz-covered baby!

Yes, fuzzed! Every inch!

He wasn't a Who,

so they called him a Grinch!

The two gals, they fed him,
and cleaned him, and oiled him.
They fussed over him—
yes, those gals really spoiled him.

The Grinch was their pride,
and the Grinch was their joy.
They treated him like
any other Who boy.

With all of his fuzz,

he was really quite cute!

Come winter, he went out…

...without a snowsuit!
Yes, life for the boy
was dandy and cool...

...until the first day of his life at Who school.

The students, they stared,
and they teased him as well.
They made fun of his fangs
and his funky Grinch smell.

The teacher, Miss Rue Who,
whose job was to teach him,
was not very good,
but she still tried to reach him.

She drummed in the lesson
that every Who knows,
from the ends of their hairs
to the tips of their toes:

Put Christmas ahead

of all other Who days.

Make Christmas your mission

in millions of ways.

Deck every hall

and shop till you drop.

Jingle those bells

and don't you DARE stop!

"Is it all really worth it?"
the Grinch had to mutter.
And then something happened
to make his heart flutter.

Young Martha May Whovier
was staring and winking.
"Could she really like me?"
the Grinch started thinking.

"Whobilation's tomorrow,"
Miss Rue Who told the gang
as she slammed the book shut
and the Who school bell rang.

"Bring in a present
for a special someWho.
Go out and shop!
Show what you can do!"

He went home and worked
with some junk that he had.
For a bunch of old junk,
it did not look so bad.

"This angel will sit
on the top of her tree.
Whenever she sees it,
she will think of me."

He found an old razor
inside an old sack.

He started to scrape
and he started to hack.

So bad was the job
that he did on his face,
the next day he hid
from the whole Whoman race.
Miss Rue Who took one look
at the Grinch and she said:
"Please take that paper bag
off of your head."

Now, August May Who
(who would one day be mayor)
liked Martha May, too,
and he did not play fair.

"This guy must be under
some kind of a curse.
The face or the gift—
I can't tell which is worse!"

The Who gang went bonkers.

They laughed and they jeered.

"August's a boss Who!"

was the cheer they all cheered.

"Your Christmas is stupid!"
the Grinch then cried out.
He started to scream
and he started to shout.
He started to jump
and he started to thrash,
until all that he touched
had been turned into trash.

So off the Grinch went
to a cave on Mt. Crumpit.
And as for the Whos,
they could like it or lump it!
He stayed in his cave
with a sneer on his face,
hating the Whos
and the whole Whoman race.

He lived all alone—

yes, these are the facts—

except for his cute

little puppy dog, Max.

So whenever the meaning
of Christmas gets hazy
and the seasonal crunch
makes you go a bit crazy,
just think of the Grinch
in his cave far away.
And remember that he
wasn't always that way.

And forget all the things
you have read or have heard.
The Grinch needs a friend,
and he needs a kind word.